THE CHOCOLATE AFFAIR

IMOGENE NIX

Edition 1 (Edible Delights) 2013

Edition 2 (Ebook only - Totally Bound) 2016

ISBN 9780648120582

Copyright © 2019 by Imogene Nix

Edition 3 (2019 Love Books Publishing)

Cover Art by Tracey at Soxsational Cover Art.

This book was previously published in two other versions and had come full circle since I wrote it back in 2012. The first was part of the Edible Delights series with Secret Cravings Publishing, then later on in E-format only with Totally Bound.

Times move on, though and the rights have finally returned to me and I'm in the position of self-publishing this book so it's under my own steam with the cover I've chosen.

Can I just say I'm totally in love with this new look?

I want to dedicate it to everyone who ever loved chocolate, because... well, you know... Chocolate! And just in case you missed it, also Pleasure Demons...

Seriously though, thank you to everyone who had a hand in the creation of the Chocolate Affair and its many incarnations. I'm pleased to be able to return it to the world and finally in print! Huzzah!

As to thanking people, my list is like a mile long! However, I must thank my long suffering husband, Mr Nix, who hung by my side when I knew there was more for this title, my daughters, the fabulous Sassie and Tracey Soxie Weston as well as Tracey W, Suzi and Keri.

Of course there is also my Mother In Law (the one everyone wants but I got) June. With much love to you!

Imogene

CHAPTER ONE

Chocolate...liters and liters of molten chocolate rolled down the conveyor belt in front of her, heading for the molds below. The sweet aroma of goodness filled her nostrils. With a rumbling stomach she turned away, knowing she had healthy food options upstairs in her office.

God I love my job! The thought never ceased to make her smile.

Sandra, from the innovations department, always laughed at her when she said that out loud. She claimed that after working here for nearly twenty years, she hated chocolate. Yet, she worked in the one part of the factory where she had to taste the chocolate confections her team designed. It was a trial for Sandra, yet Deanna could think of nothing finer.

She wrenched her mind back to the task at hand.

The new owner of Scheherazade Chocolates was due to arrive in the next hour and she needed to be sure everything was in order both down here on the manufacturing floor and upstairs in the offices.

The high quality confectionery ordered by the container load would head for the planets of *Dovan* and *Piero* taking

Scheherazade to the next level. Feliz and Alannah, the previous owners, had neither the acumen nor money to make it in the cut-throat business world, but Deanna relished the challenge of the new ownership and business model. So long as she could keep all her current staff. Once Feliz and Alannah had come to terms with the potential loss of the business, they had chosen to sell.

Scheherazade currently didn't have the capacity to increase their output. This meant anyone wishing to purchase the coveted chocolates, even in the luxurious on-world malls, had to pay premium prices for whatever was available. The new owner, a consortium with the funds to increase the output of the plant, could keep the huge overdraft. They also had the clout to deal with the administration of the planets to overcome any legislative difficulties.

Deanna looked at the plant, which she had overseen for several years. She turned back to the conveyor, looking for anything in the chocolate river that didn't belong.

Once more thoughts of Rustafan, the consortium who'd taken over the small company, intruded. She'd fretted the whole last week while reviewing policies. She'd set the workers to cleaning, but now even that was complete, leaving nothing more for her to do but wait. There wasn't much more she could do until JD Ruan, the business representative, arrived.

And what the hell kind of name was JD Ruan anyway? Deanna shrugged, a feeling of helplessness running through her.

The huge consortium now in charge of Scheherazade employed a twenty-four hour media spokesman and enjoyed a strong media profile. Yet, the heads behind the business were kept out of the spotlight—a fact that continued to intrigue her.

Try as she might, Deanna had been unable to find out who

actually owned the business. That had worried her until she realized it wasn't really important. After all, she only had to deal with the person on the ground.

With a sigh, she turned and clanked up the metal steps toward the offices.

She just hoped this JD Ruan realized she knew every aspect of running the plant and each staff member. She knew it all, right down to the carefully guarded recipes. Until now, that had made her indispensable.

Reaching for the door, she stopped in the small containment area before she pulled off the special anti-contamination socks that covered her shoes. She continued to scan the production line through the window as she shrugged off the white coat and loosened the mesh cap from her head, shaking her hair free. For a moment Deanna enjoyed the sensual pleasure as it tumbled around her shoulders.

A sound caught her attention and she turned. Whirling too quickly, she slipped on the sock where it lay discarded on the floor.

"Argh!" Arms wheeling, she tried to regain her balance but failed miserably. Strong arms reached for her as she started to fall toward the metal floor. A scent rose in her nostrils. Not chocolate, but something equally mesmerizing. Heart thudding, Deanna looked up into glittering turquoise eyes.

"Hello, what have I found here? A pleasure princess from Piero?" The voice held more than just a hint of amusement and heat scorched her cheeks.

"I don't know who you are. But this is a restricted zone." She worked to infuse censure into her words but failed, breathless in the trap of his sparkling gaze.

She couldn't focus on his words, just watched the muscular dark haired man extend a hand to her. She came to her feet and wobbled unsteadily for a moment before stepping back to take a deep breath. She caught a whiff of his musky cologne.

"And why are you supposed to be here?" Deanna's inner voice whispered to be cautious, but right now, caution was the last thing on her mind. Her body wanted to melt at the feet of this vision before her.

"I've been sent here to assess Scheherazade." He extended a long strong hand. "I'm JD Ruan."

"Oh heavens."

His first view of Deanna McCalchy had taken in the glorious lush curves and midnight hair as she shook it free of the ugly confining hat she wore. Her blue dress molded to her body while the heat of instant arousal suffused him.

Now here stood a true goddess. The thought took him by surprise. He hadn't thought in those terms for over a hundred years.

His small exclamation of interest had taken her by surprise and she had slipped. He moved with his preternatural speed extending his hands and catching her before she hit the floor.

As one of the two owners of Rustafan, he kept a low profile. He didn't want his father's minions to know where he and his sister, Entara, were. Thanks to Christabel, their media spokesperson—now his sister Entara's, lover—had ensured their anonymity. One they were grateful for.

It was a habit to hide his personal life from others. Right now, he embraced the freedom that afforded him to scan the woman in his arms, feel the weight of her body.

She watched him silently while he righted her.

"Hello, what have I found here? A pleasure princess from Piero?" Knowing that the business mainly transacted with the pleasure planets, the words slipped out. He cringed as soon as he heard them. But she didn't take offense at his words—at least not vocally, though a red tide crept over her cheeks.

"I don't know who you are. But this is a restricted zone." Her soft words of censure made him smile even as she gazed into his eyes. She was off balance, all the better for him to find out how the factory worked and maybe about her too. He shook himself mentally. That wasn't why he was here.

"That's okay, I'm supposed to be here."

"And why are you supposed to be here?" Her words betrayed her interest, but he detected no knowledge of him in her mind and let the tension release from his muscles.

"I've been sent here to assess Scheherazade." He held out one of his hands, and as she clasped it he felt a jolt of recognition, leaving him breathless for just a second. "I'm JD Ruan."

"Oh heavens." Her face pinked slightly again and he grinned, though he worked to contain his amusement at her old-fashioned comment.

"And you would have to be Deanna McCalchy?" She nodded absently.

"Yes I am. I'm sorry. I wasn't expecting you yet. Otherwise I would have met you in my office."

Deanna waved a hand toward the door into the offices. She moved with innate grace. His pulse raced as her firm backside swayed enticingly in the tunic dress. If he used any of his abilities he could no doubt have her naked on the floor in a matter of minutes, but for the first time, he felt the need to take his time. To create a real connection, not force the pleasure through her.

"Let's go to my office." With those words he followed her, watching the unconscious sway of her hips and the movement of long legs along the corridor. Her black hair swayed like water over her graceful curves. He'd be willing to bet his every credit that she was one hundred percent natural, without any toning or cosmetic touch ups that were the norm these days.

He glanced around her office once he stepped inside, pleased to take in the large, well-appointed room. He nearly sighed with pleasure at the welcoming warm, honey-tinted wood grain. The walls were dotted with her various memberships and statements of attainment. On the side of the room an image of a smiling family group surprised him and he looked again. There she stood cradling an infant. The sight snatched away his breath. *She's married!*

A quick glance at her hand showed it to be naked however. He checked the image again, and it clearly showed the glint of gold on her finger.

JD turned back to Deanna. Her purposeful steps led to a hidden door, which she touched lightly. The door swung open and he spied a small food storage unit. Reaching inside, she pulled a tray from within. The subtle waft of cool air sent the smell of chocolate throughout the room and his nostrils twitched at the scent.

"I thought we could start with a taste test of the various chocolates we make here. Give you some idea of what we produce." Her lips curved up and he smiled back, feeling the tightening of muscles at the side of his mouth.

"Indeed?" A small meeting table sat beside her desk and she lowered herself to a seat, settling the tray on the tabletop. He watched with great interest as she slipped the cover from the tray. Deanna used tiny silver tongs to place the exquisite confections on the china plate that had also been hidden on the tray.

"Try this one first. It's called Strawberry Seduction." She held the plate out toward him, which he accepted without touching her skin. Deanna had picked up hers, raising it toward her perfect pearly teeth, eyes closing in delight as she bit into the confection. The utter abandon in her enjoyment of the sweet treat fascinated him.

His insides warmed at the view before him. JD picked up the one on his plate, the small but obviously feminine chocolate figure making him smile, even as he readjusted his pants discretely. JD followed her movements, eyes closing as he smelled the chocolate, searching for the faint scent of strawberry as he bit into it. An explosion of tastes hit his tongue and he moaned. Tiny slivers of strawberry broke free from the chocolate truffle-like centre and he understood her reaction.

When he opened his eyes, she was grinning and holding out a glass of water and a dry cracker. "You need to clear your palate so you are ready for the next one." Clearly, Deanna found his reaction to be humorous. But even though he felt vexation, he couldn't find it in him the need to say anything cutting.

"Let's try the Orange Blossom Orgy next, shall we?" Her eyes twinkled and he was amazed to find they were easily read, yet he could detect nothing but the simple joy of the chocolate within them.

CHAPTER TWO

"Why do they all have such sexual names?"

"That's a really good question. They didn't used to have such adult names. They were Strawberry Explosion and Orange Crush. Somehow, though the names never really seemed right. When the pleasure planets began ordering in large quantities we decided to rename them. Given they're our biggest clients it just made sense." Deanna sat back in her chair, spine straight as if she expected an argument. From where he sat, her explanation made excellent sense.

"I like that you were considering your main audience when you renamed them." He nodded slowly. "Let's try the Orange Blossom Orgy then."

As the day rolled on, JD Ruan listened and asked intelligent questions. He stayed out of her way when she was busy, though he was always in the background. He didn't automatically make demands of the staff and waited for everyone to present the information pertaining to their roles within the company. All these things boded well for the future of Scheherazade, Deanna thought.

When the day came to an end, she gathered up her files and data chips and shoved them into the bag she stashed under her desk each morning. The small box of chocolates for tasting sat on the table and she smiled, knowing exactly what lay within. Each time she tasted one of the delightful chocolates a new flavor emerged to tease and tantalize. This one as yet remained unnamed.

Deanna reflected that this was one of the perks of her job. Feliz had been adamant that she be a lover of chocolate since she was running the factory for him. Privately, she had thought—even hoped—he would have handed the whole business to her to run for them. But Feliz and Alannah had wanted to run the company themselves with disastrous results. They'd almost bankrupted the plant before the buy-out.

Shrugging off the memories, Deanna stepped into her shoes, lovely high-heeled Du'Ca creations, moaning as her feet started to ache. She'd chosen them today because she knew the representative was coming and wanted to make a good impression. Right now, she regretted her decision.

Deanna hefted the bag over her shoulder, grunting a little as it settled into place. Home, dinner and shower followed by paperwork called. A few quick steps carried her to the door of her office. She completed her nightly routine with a final turn and blew a kiss at the image of her husband and child on the wall, then she dimmed the light and shut the door.

Quickly whirling around, she collided with a hard solid chest. "Oomph."

Gentle hands caught her bag, which began slipping off her shoulder. "Let me help." The soft breath whispered over her cheek, soft and arousing.

Deanna pulled away sharply. "It's fine."

The abrupt move left him staring at her. "Sorry. I was just coming to see you...but you're leaving."

Deanna closed her eyes, swallowing her angry tone. It wasn't his fault, she reminded herself. *No, but it was yours,* her psyche reminded her.

"No. That's fine. Yes, I was just going to go home." Her heart thudded madly and a sneaky heat crept over her skin—again. Flustered. Yes, she felt downright out of sorts and lost. It had been a long time since she had felt anything like this and it wasn't welcome. But the insidious heat continued to spiral within her belly. "If you'll excuse me?"

JD stepped away from her and coolness washed over her. "It's fine. You probably need to get home."

"I'll see you tomorrow then." It really wasn't home and hadn't been for a long time, her traitorous heart reminded her. Deanna jerked a shoulder, hoping to remind him of the work she planned to carry home.

With a short nod, he extended a hand, in wordless question but she shook her head, softening the refusal of help with a short smile.

"Well—" She stopped. What was there to say? "Goodnight, JD. I'll see you in the morning." Then with quick steps Deanna headed for the door and out into the night.

———

JD watched her hurried movements, wondering what she had to go home to. Was there a family? He would have thought so from the picture, but the lack of a ring and the late hour left him thinking that there perhaps was more to her story.

For him, a quiet evening called. He might contact his sister on Piero, where they'd agreed she should base herself, to watch over their empire while he was preoccupied here. He knew for certain he would relive the sights and sounds he had collected during the day. That alone would take some time. The emotions he'd savored though, would feed him for at least tonight. Almost as much as human food.

After a few moments he followed in Deanna's footsteps, hearing the distant sound of an engine starting, the whine of the vehicle as it moved until the sounds died away.

The large reinforced plasti-glass door of the lobby opened under his hand and he moved through, scanning the area for watchers. Finally, satisfied, JD ducked into an alley. A nod and a single murmured word were met with a loud hiss and a flash of light. The alcove disappeared and before him rose his home.

JD let out a loud hiss. Traveling anywhere on this small planet was merely a thought away, but it took magical energy that he had been unable to build up during the day.

He cast his mind back, reaching for the memory stone, where he could capture every single minute.

His first gaze of the lovely Deanna had captivated him. He'd brooded all day, while following her around. Initially his intention had been to see exactly what she knew of the business operations. If she was dead wood, he would have trimmed her away. But after today, seeing the passion and drive she exhibited, her knowledge and skill...well, he knew she would be one of the remaining staff.

The innate honesty of his kind though, forced him to also acknowledge he had also found her attractive. Arousing. Intriguing.

With a sharp epithet, he formed a vision portal to send a thought to his sister. Within seconds, she appeared in the circlet, soft and sleepy, pushing strands of black hair from her face. "Jalil al Din, how did it go?" Her soft voice settled him. He felt tight muscles begin to relax as he lowered himself to one of the overstuffed chairs.

"Good. I met the manager of the plant. We should keep

her. Find a way to promote her. She began today by introducing me to the chocolates."

Entara laughed throatily as her blue eyes sparkled. "Yes, they are truly magical pieces of craftsmanship. I have a fondness for them. But tell me, have you anything else to report? I was sleeping and would prefer to return to that state." As she smothered a long yawn, he felt a sudden jolt of concern. She was rarely tired, but if he looked carefully, he could discern lines around her eyes and mouth.

"You are well?"

She raised a hand. "Oh yes. It is just this gestation is exhausting. All is well though." A trickle of unease moved deep within his belly.

"Then I will leave you. Sleep well, sister." He smiled, working hard to ensure she could not discern his worries.

"You too, my brother."

He closed the portal, sat back and internally debated what he should do. Food, cleansing, then sleep all beckoned. Each of them would settle him for tonight's dreams.

He rose and headed for the kitchen, working to clear his mind.

———

Deanna crawled into bed. The long hours of worry had dropped away, just as they had in the weeks since JD had started at the plant.

She'd fretted about what tactics they would use to reduce staffing levels, which had been unfounded. JD seemed interested in learning about the business before making any rash decisions and with that came a calmness she'd been lacking since the takeover.

She gazed at the photo on the bedside. Every night for the past five years, she'd wished Eric and Sarah goodnight.

Five years was a long time, yet it was a ritual she felt unable to cease.

In the past it had been an emotional investment, yet tonight it felt different. It wasn't something she could put her finger on, but as she picked up the photo and kissed it, she knew *she* had changed. "Eric and Sarcha…I love you and miss you. I always will. You were such a large part of me for a long time. But I have to move on now. Find a future, somehow, without you."

Carefully, Deanna opened the drawer and saw her wedding ring lying nestled in a piece of material from Sarcha's baby blanket. She ran a soft finger over the cold metal of the ring. The burn of tears in her eyes was the worst of her reactions, she noted for the first time. Even the ache in her chest had dulled. She wondered when that had happened.

She laid the photo down on top of the ring, then slowly slid the drawer back.

Crawling into the bed, Deanna let her muscles relax, sinking into the pillowed mattress, before turning toward the middle of the bed. She pounded a large pillow into submission. Tiredness dragged at her, then her eyes dipped as sleep captured her.

The room around her was one she had never seen before. The red drapes and dim lighting a surprise. Where could she be?

A sound beside her roused her interest and Deanna turned.

On the bed beside her lay a man, his sun bronzed skin bare to the waist. She sat upright looking at the naked planes of flesh, lean and muscled. Her fingers moved of their own volition, touching the warm skin. Sliding over naked curves.

Something she hadn't felt for many years moved within her. Lust. The emotion consumed her, leaving her bewildered.

How could she feel this for a man she had only recently met? It was wrong, surely? So unfair to Eric and Sarcha.

Slowly he turned, her heart skipping a beat at the small smile on his face. "Deanna." Just the one single word burned through her. Her breath hitched as longing grew, lodging in her chest like a stone.

"JD...I haven't..."

He leaned forward, one strong hand extended toward her. He touched her, softly. "I know."

Deanna looked into his burning eyes, searching for a hint that he understood her confusion. "But JD...I haven't...I haven't done this in so long." The words ended on a moan. He smiled, drawing her closer to him for a kiss.

The kiss scorched her setting her senses aflame. "Oh JD." She leaned in, the sheet she had clutched to her breasts falling unheeded as she slipped her arms around his neck. The abrasiveness of his day's growth rasping against her sensitive skin left her hyperaware of her state of arousal.

The hand holding her hair tugged gently, as molten lava coursed through her body. His lips found the sensitive spot beneath one ear, his whispering breath teasing her beleaguered senses.

"Soft. So soft," he muttered the words causing her to shiver sensually.

Beep! Beep! Beep! The insistent sound roused her from the hot dream. The same dream had plagued her for weeks, since JD had arrived. Awareness offered no surcease from the arousal, which heated her body. She locked her legs tightly together, hoping to stem the hot wet feeling she experienced, but instead she moaned at the feeling. Her nipples engorged, becoming hard buds of sexual torture.

"No," she breathed the word no one would hear. Traitorous thoughts gathered in her mind of how she could seek release. She tried vainly to push them aside, sobbing as the need grew more insistent while the ache within her bloomed.

With a sigh, she pushed the covers aside. *It isn't supposed to be like this!*

Deanna couldn't escape the knowledge that her body needed release, as the tight spring inside her wound higher. She sighed, reaching for the hem of her nightgown. Felt it slip across her skin, grazing her breasts and hypersensitive nipples.

She used her fingers and found the springy hairs at her core, and slipped shaking fingers inwards. Felt the folds part for her questing fingers. Damp and hot. *Ready.*

"Ohh." She bent her knees slightly, shifting them further apart. Her body throbbed, more than ready for release. She closed her eyes, slipped another finger within her tight wet sheath as her thumb toyed with the hard erect bundle of nerves.

Her legs stiffened and clenched as her heart raced. "JD!" she cried out as she slipped her fingers in and out, letting her body undulate upon the bed. She slipped a hand over her satin covered breasts, stroking and rubbing the nipples, tweaking them as she sought release from the fever inside her.

More. She wanted more. Needed more. Head thrashing side to side as she increased the pace, her thumb moving faster. She worked her clit before arching up, crying out as the rhythmic spasming began.

Her body splintered and she gulped in air, struggling to fill her heaving lungs. Finally her body relaxed onto the bed as her breathing evened out again.

Deanna let her damp fingers slide free while the sense of having betrayed Eric and Sarcha strengthened. Tears leaked from tightly closed eyelids. Unable to remain in the bed any longer, she stripped the sheets and herself as if they had caused her lapse of reason. Then she collapsed in a heap on the pile of bedding, sobbing.

CHAPTER THREE

JD woke with a suddenness that spoke of some form of otherworldly intervention. He let his mind cast around for whatever caused the intrusion, yet he could sense nothing out of the ordinary. He found that strange, as he could usually feel if something or someone was near, impinging on him. At the edges of his consciousness lurked...something.

The knowledge did little to settle the growing feeling of unease though. No, he had a sneaking suspicion something waited just around the corner to surprise him. Whether the surprise was good or bad, he couldn't tell. He pushed up off the mattress, so he sat partially upright. "Nothing I can do about it."

The words dispelled the worst of the feelings, but he was certain it would only work for so long.

Crawling from the bed he reached for the glass of water, swallowing gratefully as dry membranes in his mouth absorbed the liquid. Bit by bit, his mouth lost the desiccated feel he detested while he ran an exasperated hand through his hair. Introspection wasn't something a demon usually engaged in, so what caused it this morning?

He snickered loudly, listening for the echo through the room. JD moved to the bathroom, gazing at himself in the mirror, searching for some appreciable difference.

He looked human, with his dark hair, two piercing eyes and strong though unshaven jaw. If he was honest with himself, most of the time he even felt human.

But he and his sister knew the truth. He wasn't. They weren't and had never been human.

He was a pleasure demon. It gave him great satisfaction to bring pleasure to people. Most of his clients sought sexual pleasure, something he was more than happy to indulge in with the humans who paid well for his services. It was the reason he and his sister had created the twin pleasure planets. Their exclusive resorts fulfilled the desires of their clients, assuring choice and anonymity. Not that he personally catered to them, he had a stable of males and females who adored their roles. They also eased the primal need deep within him while allowing him to keep the scruples he'd fought so long for.

And all the while his and Entara's identities remained private. It was no secret that the paternal of his species usually hunted those they sired. Not in all, to be fair, just most, in a primal need to dominate.

JD cast his mind back to his responsibilities. *Many of our clients choose the shallow road of sensual pleasure...* He pulled away from the mirror, laughing at his thoughts. "They are the clients and their every need will be accommodated," reminding himself out loud of his mantra, he entered the shower, letting the warm water sluice over his body.

His needs had always taken a backseat. Until now. He pushed away the thought of Deanna, sighing heavily as he left the stall, wrapping a towel around his waist.

JD dressed with an economy of motion before he opened a pinprick portal, searching for a safe spot as his destination.

With a word, then a movement, time and space folded around him.

On arrival at the plant, he stood, still and silent, listening for anything that may have witnessed his movements. The rumble of a vehicle engine sounded and the play of headlights cut through the gloom. He waited several seconds before stepping into the bright beams, before they flicked off.

"You're early." Deanna's voice, falsely bright greeted him.

"Business never sleeps. You have to be early to win the prize." The words rolled off his tongue as his gaze scoured her face.

She'd experienced a bad night. She may as well have written it on her face. No amount of cosmetics could hide the ravages of pink eyes, swollen from crying or the dark circles below.

"Come on, then. Since you're here, we may as well get started." She bit the words out as she juggled her heavy bag. On the tip of his tongue was an offer to take the load but something in her stance, tense and on edge, told him not to offer.

Instead he trudged behind her, watching as she swiped her security card through the reader to open the front doors. "I'll meet you in your office in around ten minutes." Deanna dismissed him at the entrance to the suite of offices, padding away as he watched her.

Something had upset her overnight, surprise and anger filled him. The emotions both unfamiliar and unwelcome.

The whole morning passed in a haze of self-recriminations. She shouldn't have given in to the urges that woke her.

Deanna tried to paper over her self-anger with the excuse

of the mountains of work that needed completing but her conscience nipped and bit at her.

Every file she opened dealt with pleasure of some form, reinforcing the choice she had made, and grating on her already raw nerves. She kept reliving the decision to give in and self-pleasure. One she bitterly regretted now. Each new issue—from staffing to ordering—increased her anger at herself, fanning the flames roiling within her belly.

She snapped at staff when they buzzed, grouched at the coffee machine and stalked through the corridors. By lunchtime, her temper had frayed enough that everyone in the office walked wide circles around her.

It seemed inconceivable that having given into the need, she now experienced an anger that left her at odds with everyone, including herself. She slammed the file back to the desk, letting out an irritated sound, before rubbing her brow. Thoughts of her own choices rode her without mercy.

The door opened and Deanna opened her mouth to deliver a blistering set down as JD entered. She swallowed her angry words as he slipped inside, shutting the door softly behind him.

"According to your staff, this is unfamiliar behavior for you." JD indicated at the untidy piles of files with a small smile. "Now, how about you and I take a lunch break while you tell me about what has you using the staff as chew toys." He softened the words with a smile and she groaned inwardly.

Nice going Deanna. Way to make the boss think you're incapable of running the show when he leaves.

Deanna rose, ready to apologize for her unprofessional behavior, but instead found him beside her. His hand slipped under her elbow and gently guided her to the door. With no other choice, except to look foolish, she accepted his guidance to the front door. During the short walk, she thought through her actions during the day so far. Her introspection made her stomach churn nervously.

A luxury transport vehicle waited beyond the door and JD smiled, stopping her short. *How and why?* The question swirled as he indicated that she should precede him within.

With a small, silent nod, she climbed into the large vehicle, noting the plush interior. The padded white seats, darkly tinted glass and soft piped music felt amazingly decadent. A silver ice bucket nestled in a corner, bearing a bottle of champagne, which she knew cost a lot of credits from the quick glance at the label. JD climbed in beside her and the door shut. She breathed deeply, hoping to calm her nerves.

Last night's dream kept playing over and over in her mind —especially his starring role—and his proximity played havoc with her nerves. She wanted to touch him, a thoroughly unusual reaction for her. Instead, she straightened her spine and scootched a little further away, closing her eyes in self-disgust.

Right. Like he has the same problem I do—unrequited lust for nondescript little me. Ha! He's so gorgeous, he could probably get any woman he wants. You, Deanna, don't even make the cut. Even Eric, her husband of five years had called her interesting, rather than beautiful.

The vehicle moved, with vibrations so slight she almost missed them as they pulled into the traffic. Deanna watched the cars traveling around them, while battling to regain her equilibrium.

"So, I'm thinking lunch and a glass of wine to give you time to mellow." His hand waved through the air as Deanna restrained the urge to roll her eyes at his languid voice. "Then you tell me what is bothering you today."

"I, um—" Deanna stopped as they pulled into the marina. "Where are we going?" Her head whipped around and she saw JD smile with a hint of devilry as she made to explain why they couldn't have lunch here.

"To my boat, which will take us somewhere we can talk. Undisturbed. There is only the captain. Once we get to our destination, he and the chef will make themselves scarce." She opened her mouth again while his face sobered. "Look, something has been riding you all day, and the entire office is treading carefully. They're afraid they're going to fall through the thin ice you're burying us in." A gentle hand touched her knee and she nearly jerked in reaction.

His comment about what was riding her, unintentional or not, nearly sent her blood pressure through the roof. Raunchy visions invaded her mind at his words. They were not what he had in mind, she was sure. So Deanna breathed shallowly, hoping to dispel the memories that turned her knees to water, and filled her with a burning need.

The door opened and he alighted. She stepped out, straight into his arms. The slide of his clad body against hers ratcheted up the emotions that churned inside her belly. She sucked in a breath, ready to ask him to let her go, but instead his scent enveloped her.

———

Arousal. It might be brief and passing, but he could smell the enticing scent on her. He sniffed the air unconsciously as the musky scent washed off her in waves. His gut reacted instinctively, the muscles in his back tightened live wire wound around a stake, and as much as he attempted to ignore the pull of desire he couldn't. Sweat poured from his body and his cock swelled in reaction.

I might be a pleasure demon, but my role is to ensure others feel pleasure, not to take it for myself. But once more his own body betrayed him.

JD stepped back from Deanna, his keen eyesight taking in the overly bright glint in her eye, and the shallow breathing. The hint of a blush on her cheeks flagged her need. His heart beat a rapid tattoo at the thought.

Torture. Lunch would be sheer torture, he acknowledged, guiding her carefully up the gangway to the fast tender that would take them to his hideaway.

The captain waved from the bridge once they were aboard and he hurried Deanna to a chair. "We need to buckle in. This boat moves very fast." No sooner had he said the words than the hum of the engine split the air. He took the seat next to her. The boat pulled away slowly at first, but quickly gathered speed while he watched the plumes of spray from the bow. He hoped the ride would settle the internal struggle within himself.

The journey was swift. Before long he could feel the engines slowing while the wash started settling. The boat swayed slightly, pulling up to a small jetty.

"Where are we?" Her voice quavered a little and he chanced a look. Deanna was hanging onto the side of her chair, looking pale and slightly green. JD cursed, making her seasick wasn't in his plan.

He slipped his hand over hers and felt her grip his fingers as calmness descended within him.

The captain came forward quietly to inform them they could disembark. As they stood, he noted Deanna remained a little unsteady. He automatically moved behind her, slipping an arm around her small waist. The heat of her burned him, while his inner demon reveled in the sensations coursing through his body.

Together they left the boat heading up the gangplank. He watched as she looked around her. "Where are we?" He realized he hadn't answered the previous question.

"A'Vianca."

Gaping at him, she whispered, "But that's like super exclusive. Even when Feliz and Alannah were considered the best of the best in the chocolate world, they couldn't get reservations!"

He smiled. She didn't yet know the corporation owned the small island in the middle of the ocean. "Well, sometimes you just need to know someone, who knows someone." She looked shocked as he winked, ushering her within the interior of the small floating resort style building.

Once inside, she stopped and he watched her take everything in. The subtle whites as they merged with greens and blues. The barely there tones had been chosen to relax and entice.

They were rooms that reminded you of sin, with heavy brocade curtains and large four- poster beds. One in particular he didn't want her to see.

At least, not yet.

"I really don't think…" Her voice carried a lost quality and he wondered if his plan hadn't been a little overkill, after all. But they were here and he would make the best of his decision.

JD leaned in close to her ear. "Then don't." Pulling away was the hardest thing he had done as his chest tightened with need. He hadn't come here to engage in a sexual frolic. He could see it wasn't what she wanted. But he had caught her scent, lightly floral, a touch of sweetness, and breathing in had made him ache painfully.

He indicated the private setting, hidden from the public areas. Shining wine glasses sitting on pristine white linen, teamed with fine china and silverware. They gleamed in the light and a burst of pride filled him. JD pulled out a chair and Deanna sank down gracefully to the padded seat.

"So…" She watched him with her slate gray eyes. "Where do you want to start?"

JD watched her eyes. He noted how the droop remained at the corner of her mouth. "You tell me."

"I've had a bad day and taken my anger out on the staff. Something that is both inappropriate and unprofessional. It's not like me usually. But..." Her eyes slid away from his while a blush rimmed her cheeks. "I can't even begin to give you an explanation of why. Just that I know it was wrong."

Unease slithered through him, greasy and oily. The emotion wrapped around his belly. "This isn't a session to tell you to ease off. I just wanted to give you a way out, so you can settle before returning to the office, or head home. It's Friday and, after lunch, an early day is certainly understandable."

Deanna obviously wasn't going to calmly accede to his suggestion, he noted. Her mouth opened, ready to dismiss the comment, but he raised a hand.

"I can see something has upset you, so can the staff. Your mood today isn't conducive to a calm workplace. My hope is you can either share your concerns with me...or at least come to terms with them. But let's eat first. I always find a good meal improves a person's outlook."

She didn't return the smile, only grimaced, and he mentally shrugged. He was doing everything he could to help her come to terms with whatever bedeviled her. But she still looked unhappy with dark shadows lurking in her eyes, and her drooping lips.

"I didn't mean to react like I have today. I just have...some issues," she whispered quietly. For the first time he could see the sorrow that enveloped her.

"Want to tell me about it?" He stayed still, waiting and watching.

"How about I tell you over lunch?"

He noted the swing of the doors as the single server advanced with their entrees and wanted to growl with dissatisfaction. But the reaction would be unfair. They were simply doing their job.

Plates were laid before them, the fine silver domes removed with a minimum of drama, thankfully. A quiet query about drinks followed. They too were served quickly from a bottle sourced beyond the doors, and then silence reigned once more.

Deanna lifted a fork, then began picking at the deep fried sesame prawns on a bed of fresh crisp greens. "I was married. With a daughter…" He listened as she wove the tail of love that brought her and her late husband, Eric, together. How they had married with much fanfare and the birth of their eagerly awaited daughter, Sarcha.

"She was only six. It was her birthday." Deanna's face paled further. He yearned to reach out and hold her hand. Instead he ignored the need that arced through him. She looked up at him, her eyes shining with tears. "I was working on a new project and couldn't get to her party. They messaged me afterward. They were on their way home. I said…" She stopped, breathing deeply and he felt a crushing pain in his chest.

This tale has to end badly. He held himself still, waiting.

"I said I'd be there when I could get away. I said I was really busy. There was an accident on the way home. They both died." Her words were almost inaudible now.

JD ached for her. "When did this happen?" She needed to talk he knew, seeing the way she held her hand to her chest, as if the pain were fighting to break free. JD wondered if she'd bottled all her emotions up since then.

"Five years ago." A single tear slipped down her face.

"Have you discussed this with anyone else?"

She shook her head, wisps of hair flying free from the casual knot she'd chosen today.

"Why not?"

Deanna shrugged without a word dropping her gaze. "I said goodbye last night. Put their photo away." The whispered words finally had the last piece clicking into place in his mind.

"Oh, Deanna." The need to soothe roared through him while she coughed, sniffled and tears rolled down her face.

He stood, moving beside her before he sank to the floor, opening his arms, which he folded around her. Her paroxysm of grief washed over him, leaving him at war with his desire for the woman in his arms. He held still, though, letting her free the pain and anguish she had bottled up.

When the storm of emotion passed, she shared a small sad smile. "You must think I'm crazy." She lifted her swollen eyes to his. He shook his head.

"No. I think you are the most beautiful woman I have ever seen."

Her eyes widened, then she pulled away.

CHAPTER FOUR

"I'm not beautiful. I've got puffy eyes and a red nose, I'm sure." Deanna groped for her bag, looking for something to wipe and blow with. But the more she hunted the more likely it became that she would turn up with nothing.

"Here." His soft words had her looking at him, as he extended a snowy white handkerchief.

"Thanks." She gratefully grabbed the cloth and dabbed at her eyes and cheeks before turning to blow. *How much more humiliating can this get?* Deanna composed herself before turning back to him. She saw him, still kneeling next to her chair as she leaned forward.

She only meant to kiss him on the cheek, but at the last second he moved and her lips touched his.

Electric.

Nothing else came to mind then as need and heat took over. The kiss deepened with his mouth opening over hers. Their tongues touched, tip to tip. His hands moved, their grip firming over her shoulders before pushing aside material so his fingers touched her skin.

Bang!

Deanna pulled back at the sound, seeing the doors to the kitchen swinging open and moaned. *Oh God! I've just engaged in a passionate make out session with my boss!*

Enjoyable though the embrace had been, the truth didn't change who or what he was. Her boss. *What must he think of me?*

Her face flamed as she hurriedly adjusted her clothing, hoping the server wouldn't notice. A vain hope, as he avoided looking at either of them while he went about his business. Deanna snuck a glance at JD who stood with his back to her, but the movements betrayed his actions as he tore off his tie.

Damn it. I don't even know his first name, only his JD moniker. No, for all I know, he's high up in the consortium, or married. He looks like sin and I just had my tongue halfway down his throat. She dropped her head again, knowing she'd struggle to look at him the same way again.

A sound caught her attention forcing her to look up. JD settled himself back in front of her a small smile on his lips.

"Well. That was embarrassing." As he laughed at her words, she was unable to control the small giggle that escaped.

"Now though, I suggest we eat this lovely meal before it goes to waste. Then we can talk, properly. How does that sound to you?"

The churning in her belly subsided slightly while she tackled her omelet, surprised to find crabmeat, ginger and even snow peas. She moaned again as flavors exploded in her mouth. "I haven't had anything this good for a long time."

"No, I can't say I have either, except when I was involved in these negotiations once..." A funny anecdote ensued. Deanna found herself laughing at his witty repartee while they finished lunch, then a light sorbet was wheeled out.

By the end of the meal, she sat, one hand on her stomach

feeling better than she had for years. "Gee, I feel totally stuffed and quite lazy in fact."

"Then let's relax a little. Enjoy the company."

For a moment Deanna weighed going back to work, where she'd hidden since the death of Sarcha and Eric, then shrugged the feelings off. Working seven days a week for so long meant she could take a couple of hours to herself.

In the back of her mind, she knew it was because she wanted more. Her subconscious whispered that she needed the sensual touch of this man.

Instead Deanna stood and trailed behind him, to a small sitting area, carefully shaded but with a magnificent view of the blue ocean. She looked out to see the empty jetty. "Where's the boat?"

"It's moored at the back of the island where the staff will remain until we call for them." He poured her another white wine. After accepting the glass, she sipped the tangy liquid, building up her courage to ask the one question burning inside her.

Taking in a deep breath, she turned to see him watching her. "JD...I want to ask..." She stopped unable to say the words. He smiled.

"My name is Jalil al Din. But you can just call me Jalil." He set her glass on the table beside him and moved closer to her before extending a hand. "Say my name, Deanna."

"Jalil al Din." She put all her longing into the words as he moved closer to her. Her breath hitched.

"Be sure you want this." His eyes burned into her. She had never before wanted something, quite the way she wanted this connection.

"I want everything." She moved into his arms, their lips touching tenderly this time. And she gloried in their mutual desire.

———

Deanna melted into his arms, twining her fingers at the back of his neck, enjoying how his supple lips moved over hers. Not demanding but seeking permission to enter. Each caress grazed her quivering flesh lightly, like the skip of a dancing flame.

She slid her hands over the suit he wore. The urgency to feel his skin once more called. She moved away slightly, watching his turquoise eyes as her fingers found the buttons, first to his jacket, then his shirt. His skin, naturally bronzed felt warm. She shivered taking in the dark flat nipples, the sculptured abs and the densely packed muscles of his arms.

Deanna couldn't help herself. "You are so beautiful." His eyes darkened further as she tentatively leaned into him. She touched her mouth to the cording at his shoulders. She could feel him shiver beneath her light caress.

Soft hands stopped her from moving, then dropped to carefully find the concealed clips holding her blouse together. She arched, offering him everything and exhaled as clips gave. The blouse draped open for him to see all of her. Deep within, her stomach churned as if it were the consistency of warm chocolate cascading through her nervous system. Her limbs weighing heavily, she now wanted to close her eyes with the sheer pleasure of the moment.

"Lift your arms." His quiet words were met with the touch of his mouth once more upon her lips. She gave him access as she mewled her pleasure.

The material slipped from her shoulders while his strong arms folded around her waist drawing her against him. The feel of flesh on flesh was magic. Her whole body tingled with sensations she had never felt before, leaving her breathless and gasping.

"Oh God!" Her head tipped back as his lips found the

sensitive spot below her ear. Clever fingers moved over her back, loosening the black bra that confined her breasts. Finally, they too sprang loose as he slipped the straps down her arms, while his mouth ravaged her collarbone. The tiny licks and kisses stealing her capacity to think.

Deanna lifted her heavy arms, tracing the lines of his chest before finding her way to the clips, buttons and zips that held his suit pants in place. She fumbled, chest heaving with exertion, reveling in the web of sensuality he wove around her with such skill.

Now free of the confines of the lacy bra, her nipples grazed the skin of his chest, puckering to hard points of pleasure and she cried out again. His voice whispered words she couldn't understand, but the intention in them infinitely clear. Softly said, they continued to arouse her.

Her skirt melted away beneath his ministrations. She felt the fingers hook beneath the elastic of her panties, where they roamed slowly. Her hips gyrated unconsciously as her core ached with need. Deanna gasped again as fingertips brushed the mound hidden below and she bucked.

She moved her hands back to his pants pushing them away together with the briefs, which had been hidden below, until his cock sprang free. The clothing hit the floor with a thud, which they both ignored. After a quick toeing motion removed his shoes, he slipped the pants from his feet.

"I can't wait to feel you." His accented words, so alien and unfamiliar left her shivering in reaction. "To fill you. To taste you even."

Her mouth opened in silent supplication, feeling as if he were devouring her with his open-mouthed kisses, drugging her as they moved down her body. His fingers delved below the layer of lace that hid her core from his view.

"Please...Jalil..." Her broken words seemed to spur him into action as he swooped forward and hooked his arm under her legs, bringing her out of the sexual stupor. "Where are you taking me?"

"Somewhere infinitely more comfortable."

Deanna shivered again, this time in response to the promise of his words. Her mind churned slowly as he carried her from the room then down a hallway before entering another room.

The bedroom existed for sin and debauchery her mind warned. JD lay her down on the white lace coverlet. She sank into the comfort of the bed while he stripped her panties from her, she realized dimly that her shoes had somehow been discarded in the thrilling interlude previously. Then her thoughts fled.

JD climbed onto the bed, the look in his eyes feral with primitive need. In his gaze she caught a flash of something before his lips found her ankle. His hands circled her flesh as he nuzzled her foot. Never before had someone touching her foot left her breathless, but his ministrations continued, his lips quested from her ankle to her calf while she gripped the coverlet. "Jalil...I need you..." Her broken words were answered with a small laugh.

"Soon, my beauty. But your pleasure must come first." Her heart raced in her chest as she felt the molten touch at her knees, then moving farther up. His tongue laved the skin of her inner thigh and she quaked, knowing she would come before he joined her. She grasped her breast with one hand, plucking, while the other sought his hair. On finding the silky strands, she twined her fingers as his mouth finally closed over her cleft.

"Ahhh..." she cried out at the feel of him. His tongue found its way between her folds, moving back and forth while two fingers pushed their way within.

"Oh God!" she shouted, her legs moving as the roiling burning feeling enveloped her, pushing her to orgasm.

She panted as her body eased back down. The thumping of her heart ceased its mad race. Opening her eyes, she stared at the ceiling before realizing she still had a hold of his hair.

"Jalil?" she asked, releasing him.

"What?" She could hear his heavy breathing and looked down. Jalil's beautiful eyes were hooded. She knew what to do. Carefully sitting up, she smiled, then extended a shaky hand.

"Come here."

He didn't move so she clambered to her knees and hands. "Well now, it's not fair for me to have all the fun. You shouldn't have to miss out." Sparks flashed in his eyes and she grinned.

"Deanna..." His hesitant words didn't stop her as she crawled forward, all inhibitions gone.

She reached him in the middle of the bed, then slipped her hands over his damp skin.

"No...you don't understand."

Deanna didn't give him time for anymore words as her lips found his, deepening the kiss. He tasted musky and inviting. His lips still tasted of her.

She pushed him back to the coverlet and followed him down. Sliding her hands over his body, she sought his stiff cock before lovingly encircling the engorged shaft. A quick pump had him moving in time with her. Triumph roared through her as she moved her body against his. As she straddled him, the rasp of his nipples against her naked skin left her breathless as she grew warm once more, her body readying itself for the ultimate invasion.

"I want you. I want everything." Even as she spoke, Deanna lowered herself, feeling the scorching tip at the entrance to her core. "I want it all." The final words were a whisper as she impaled herself, ending with a hiss.

Strong hands clamped around her hips, pushing her more

firmly down as she lost herself once more in the rush of sensations. She nudged her hips as he seated himself all the way within her, and she moaned.

He wasn't gentle now, urging her to move faster as she bucked. "Give me everything, Deanna." His guttural words a command she couldn't ignore as she rode him, hard and fast. Moving up and down on his steely rod, she was soon as damp as him, their bodies slick with sweat. She gripped his shoulders seeking purchase as her heart thudded.

"More!" Deanna chanted, challenging him.

With a final thrust, she splintered in his arms and he cried out. "Everything!" One last shuddering movement seated him far within her as he jetted his seed. They stayed suspended, bodies milking the moment before they slowly collapsed into each other.

JD's eyes flashed open. "Oh. My. God."

Deanna looked up into his face to see horror. "JD?"

"What have I done?"

CHAPTER FIVE

As soon as the words escaped he wanted to call them back. She moved away from him leaving his body cool. *Damn. Did I really say that out loud?* But one look at the hurt on her face, her eyes shining with tears taunted him. *Yes, I did.*

"Deanna...I..." *But what can I say?*

She raised a shaking hand and shook her head. "Don't." Her voice wobbled and he felt even lower.

She crawled awkwardly to the edge of the bed and got off, pulling the coverlet with her. "I'm going to get my clothes, then I think I should go." Seeing the hollowness in her eyes, he tried to capture her arm as she passed by.

"Don't touch me." She whirled on him. "You wine me, dine me and think I'll jump into your bed? Then when you get what you want..." She threw a hand into the air, swiping at her burning cheeks as he watched. Fascination flared even though he didn't want it, as the tide of pink rose on her face. "Go. To. Hell." Once more she moved swiftly, but the comforter made her movements awkward. She slipped, both hands reached for empty air as she dropped her covering. He grabbed her, mere inches from the floor.

"Damn it. Give me a chance to explain," he muttered as she wriggled in his grasp.

"I don't want to hear what you have to say." But the fire had retreated from her voice. Instead he heard it wobble as he pulled her tightly against himself. Waves of pain radiated from her and his chest ached at the anguish he'd caused with his lack of thought and control.

"No. This is important, Deanna." He swung her up in his arms before retreating to the bed. Now she waited, stiff and silent. "I need to tell you about me."

He gulped, seeing the small red mark slowly emerging on her skin. *It's too late not to tell her the truth.* But only the whole, unvarnished truth would work. "I am...not...umm..." His stomach roiled and he feared her reaction. She probably won't take this well.

"I'm not human," he said the words, waiting for her response.

She snorted, throwing her head back. "You expect me to believe that? Fine. The fairy in space is real too." She swung her face away from him. He couldn't take back his words now.

"No. You see...I'm a demon. A pleasure demon." "Yeah. Like I've ever heard of a pleasure demon. At least it's an original title." He winced, then forged on. "I am. Our role is to ensure humans enjoy...umm...experience pleasure. It is our reason for being. My sister Entara and I...we own the pleasure planets and the consortium. We don't broadcast that information, because of what we are."

Deanna snorted, determinedly facing away from him and JD gave into the urge to touch her, placing a gentle finger under her chin and turning it toward him. Hot tears rolled down her face. "Let me show you."

"Show me what?"

This time his resolve was firm as he allowed his body to

assume its natural form. He remained the same size and shape, except with mottled, green and blue hued skin and his eyes a reddish brown. She gasped, pulling away.

"What are you?"

Fear.

JD could hear the dark emotion in her voice for the first time. Anger curled through him.

"I'm still me." His voice became deeper and gruffer. She growled at his words. As she cringed, he gave up. "I'll leave you."

JD stood up, letting his body return to the human color he usually assumed. His legs taking him quickly across the room, and he extended his hand to the door handle...

"Wait!" He stopped, heart pounding. "Will I—" She stopped and he tensed. "Can I...get pregnant?" Her soft words pierced him to the heart.

"Only if..." He swallowed, his imagination bringing up an image of her large with child. "Only if you have demon blood." Then he wrenched open the door and left the room.

CHAPTER SIX

Deanna waited only long enough for Jalil to pass her the clothes through a crack in the door before she scurried into them. Checking the mirror of the small ensuite attached to the bedroom. She couldn't ignore that her hair and makeup were a mess, and much as she might want to request her bag, she dared not. It was all to embarrassing! Instead she hid, reasoning the less time together, the easier to avoid him.

Occupying herself, she washed away her makeup and the streaks of mascara that trailed down her face, then finger combed her hair. The whole time she tried to ignore the just tumbled look on her face. But she failed. She didn't have to see herself in the mirror to know the truth. She could still feel the small daylong growth grazes on her skin together with the subtle swelling of her lips from his hungry kisses. Kisses she desperately wanted to forget.

With a final shrug she left the bathroom, studiously avoiding looking at the bed, rumpled from their intimacy. The comforter lay discarded on the floor.

She yanked on the door, the cold of the handle barely making an impression before she stalked down the hallway to find him standing at the window, staring out at the water. His shoulders slumped while his hands were thrust deeply into his trouser pockets. A seed of disquiet grew inside, but she ignored the emotion. Instead she looked for her bag, seeing where the leather lay on the floor beside the table. Deanna reached for the handles and swung them over her shoulder. "I'm ready to leave now."

He nodded without a word, then turned away, heading to the swinging doors. She waited by the door, her muscles tense. As he returned, a sound filled the air. The launch they arrived on returned to the jetty.

The sleek machine she would never normally have boarded willingly, waited. In silence Jalil opened the door, then ushered her forward. She stepped lightly along the weathered boards.

He offered an arm as she went to climb onto the boat, but she ignored his help, thinking to manage by herself as she gripped the side. The vessel moved, bouncing against the walkway, then away with a thud.

Unable to find purchase, Deanna nearly fell to the water, but his hand caught her. JD steadied her, then lifted her aboard the craft.

"Thank you." He nodded in silence.

Everything felt so wrong! The first man she had any attachment to since Eric, wasn't even a man! She clamped viciously down on the emotions whirling through her, once more resuming her seat and clipping the belt into place as she settled into the seat. The engine roared as the boat pulled away and turned sharply making her grip the seat as her stomach rolled. Traveling on water really wasn't something she enjoyed. At least her uncertain stomach kept her mind off the turmoil within her in the wake of the brief interlude between them.

The small floating island moved further away, becoming

no more than a speck on the horizon, while plumes of spray danced. Deanna hoped to keep her mind occupied from how she would deal with the mess she had made. Sadness sat like a heavy stone in her belly. She sniffed, attempting to keep the tears at bay, once more.

Soon the boat began to slow and Deanna was thankful as her stomach heaved unmercifully. If the ride had lasted much longer she would have been dreadfully sick. She didn't miss the irony though. Truly, the lesser of the evils had been traveling by boat. The thought nearly overwhelmed her.

She moved swiftly looking for the vehicle they had arrived in, unsurprised when the car drew to a silent stop in front of her. She managed to ignore Jalil for now and hoped to continue to do so until they reached the factory. The ride took place in silence, as she looked out the car window, shutting him out as effectively as possible.

When they pulled into the driveway his fingers covered hers on the metal door handle. "Deanna, we really must talk."

She wrenched her hand away, but the echo of his touch left her senses reeling. "I really don't want to."

He shrugged as he opened the door, stepped to the side as she clambered out, and then shut the door. Deanna took advantage of his preoccupation and headed for her car, climbing in as swiftly as she could, punching the engage button before tearing out of the car park. But as she merged into the evening traffic, she looked back, seeing him watch her in the mirror.

The trip home was horrendous as her mind kept replaying their lovemaking. Tears trickled down her face. I've made such a mess of the situation. "Damn it, I know better than to sleep with a co-worker. Or even boss!" She moaned as she parked close to her small apartment on the ground floor. Thankfully the hour was late enough. She knew most of the residents were already settled safely inside. Deanna scrambled for her door, unlocking the safety latches before dashing within.

The dark gloomy interior matched her mood as she threw her bag to the side, then stumbled for the bedroom. She quickly stripped off her clothes, which smelled of him. They also reeked of sex.

She caught sight of the unmade bed but veered away, letting the tears fall freely now. All she wanted was to cleanse her body and soul.

———

The lights from her vehicle had disappeared into the distance but he waited. *I've gone about this all wrong.* He kicked a stone, watching absently as it rose into the air, before falling on the other side of the road.

Shaking his head, he looked for a dark area to mask him as he disappeared. A thought and sound took him back to the island. Standing within the small sunroom, he sniffed. The scent of their lovemaking remained in the air, reminding him of the intense pleasure he had experienced. *Did humans always experience such pleasure in loving?* He shook his head. "I'm not human, so I wouldn't know." His self-deprecating words echoed in the silence.

The door at the end of the building swung open. "Did you wish for something, sir?" The young woman who acted as chef inquired and he shook his head.

He waited for the girl to retreat to the staff work and living area. Right now he wanted nothing except silence. He needed to be able to lick his wounds in solitude. He conjured up a glass of red wine and his memory ball, taking a deep draught as he lowered himself into the deep seat.

Alone with his thoughts, he realized she had been tight and ready. He hoped to heaven he wasn't her first experience since the death of her husband but the thought niggled at him. He finished the wine before he placed the glass on the small coffee table and opened a portal.

Entara sat, wide awake this time, smiling as she saw him. "Greetings, brother. I hope you have some glad tidings for me."

He shook his head. "No, but I do need some advice."

Her eyes softened. "So, you have found the one, then?"

He sat up straighter in his chair, startled. *The One?*

Dear Heaven, if she is the one, I have a very big problem on my hands. His stomach revolted at the thought. A human, maybe The One being in his whole long lifetime that could join her life force to his. Share his long lonely journey through life.

As soon as Entara muttered the words, his mind thought back. The small mark on her back. The way the red patch had glowed as she tried to get away from him.

A lump formed in his throat. "I have a problem." The happy face became sober. "What have you done?" He quickly recounted the scene as she closed her eyes. The truth now seemed so much worse than he had imagined. "I don't know what you're going to do. You have only forty-eight hours to rectify the situation. It's not a lot of time to gain her agreement to the bonding." Her soft voice sounded sad, reinforcing what he already knew.

He needed a miracle for the situation to be resolved.

"Do you wish me to come to you?" Entara stood slowly. For the first time he could see how heavy she had become.

"No. You must remain there, under Christabel's care. At least until you have birthed."

She shook her head. "But you have need of me." Through the centuries, he and his twin had been inseparable. But now she carried her own offspring, requiring constant care and the attention of her mate. Many of their kind experienced difficult gestations and births.

"No. You stay. I'll make it right. Somehow." She smiled but he could see she didn't believe his words as he ended the conversation, then closed the portal.

Unable to prevent himself, he headed down the corridor, stopping at the first door. The coverlet remained on the floor. He picked up the heavy blanket, inhaling deeply. Her scent, light and sweet remained on the fabric. He hauled it close, seeking comfort as he dragged it out into the corridor, heading to his own room. The red drapes and covers now felt like an insult as he flung himself to the bed, pulling the scented coverlet over himself.

Jalil lay still, looking at the plain ceiling. Ideas flashed through his mind, one after another.

He could go to her. He could grovel. Perhaps offer her ownership of Scheherazade? He knew his sister would not fuss. Yet no action felt right. Another thought formed in his mind.

She had to sleep. Perhaps in a dream visitation he could promote the healing between them? He only had forty-eight hours. He needed to use the time wisely.

Altering his consciousness, he sought the dreaming plane. Once there, he searched. With each dream he entered, he became more despondent. Just as he prepared to give up hope, he found her.

He gazed down at Deanna as she lay on her bed. She was truly lovely. Jalil touched her forehead.

"Deanna?" She looked at him with distaste and anger.

"How did you get here?" Her words were tight. The signs of misery still showed clearly. Her eyes were red rimmed and her skin an unnatural shade of red, as if she had scrubbed to clean her body.

"I came through the dream plane. I needed to see you. To explain." He hoped she would let him, but understood she could force him out.

"But what if I don't want you to?" She looked away.

He felt the loss keenly. He only had one chance now. He needed to make the best possible case.

"Deanna, I have come to care about you, in so many ways. But now I have a problem." He reached out a hand, taking hers gently, holding it close. This time, she didn't pull away, but waited, watching him as if she didn't quite trust anything he said.

"Tell me your problem." She sighed and he felt a lightening of the load on his chest. She would listen. He couldn't ask any more, right now.

"Did you notice a red mark on your back this evening?" His voice was strangled, but he continued. If she had indeed found the mark, then he needed her to make a decision quickly. His whole future depended on her actions.

"I...well, yes. I wondered about it. It wasn't there before we...well, you know. Had sex." Her truculent tones admonished him. "It's between my shoulder blades. Why?" Her question was blunt.

"Because it seems you have been marked as my One. We demons may only have one life mate, who can join their life force to us. A large round red mark appears after lovemaking." Deanna quirked an eyebrow at his choice of wording, but didn't interrupt. "As you now seem to have that mark, I assume you are my mate."

"What does this mark mean exactly?" Suspicion colored her tone.

He wanted to smash his hand against the wall. The damage he had done with his stupid comments were more far reaching than he could have imagined.

"Either I bond to you, or I will never be able to be whole again."

She slumped back looking at him with a horrified expression. "You have to be kidding? Right?"

CHAPTER SEVEN

Deanna woke with a start, looking around wildly as her heart rhythm settled. Her hands searched, seeking something that plainly wasn't there, while she raged inwardly at his intrusion in her dreams. How could he do this to her! *How the hell could he even be in my dream?*

With jerky movements she threw the bed covers out of the way as she clambered out. A sound from the corner intruded on the silence while a flash of light startled her, nearly blinding in intensity before it disappeared. There stood Jalil. He stepped forward as she gasped, backing away at the intrusion.

"Get out." Her voice vibrated with anger in the silence as he stalked toward her. "No. We need to sort this out now. Rationally." The fire in her chest grew. "Rationally? Let's see then, shall we?" She inhaled and squared her shoulders. "You hid who you were. You hid *what* you were. You also knew I was vulnerable. Yet, you still took advantage. Sure, let's do rational, shall we?"

She illustrated each statement with a poking finger, stabbing at the air between them. Dimly, she noted how he winced as her words dripped with icy coldness.

"None of it was on purpose. I never meant to…" His hands outstretched, he beseeched her to understand his position, but right now, no middle ground existed for her. The pain in her chest, the sense of betrayal crowded everything else out.

He stood watching her, his hand dropping to his side limply as he spoke softly. "I'm sorry. I don't know what more to say." He shrugged. Defeat oozed from him.

She saw it in his eyes, as well as pain.

"I want to make you realize that I never—" He stopped.

His adam's apples bobbed up and down as he swallowed.

A chink opened in her heart at the despair in his actions. Deanna struggled vainly, wanting to keep the hurt and anger close. She sought to use the fury within her as a shield against him. But his sorrow and remorse tore at her.

What if it was truly unintended? *What if he's genuinely sorry? Just because I'm in pain, should I throw away any chance at hope? What if I could be happy again?* Don't go there.

But it was too late to go back now.

"I don't know." Her eyes burned as the conflicting thoughts chased around in her mind, leaving her lost in the maelstrom.

"Time. It's going to take time." She ran shaking fingers through her hair even as she closed her eyes.

"I don't have time. That's the problem."

Deanna opened her eyes as he grimaced. She felt a spurt of anger again at his words. Only this time, there wasn't the intensity that had been there before.

She wasn't the one who had put him in this position. It was his actions that had created the mess. But she recognized her thoughts as unfair.

He'd said there could be no going back. Jalil had sought her consent, which she had willingly given.

Do I want to be alone forever? "Look. I want to change and —" She stopped as thoughts came. Then what? The mess between them would spill over into the workplace. It had to. Damn! Given he owned Scheherazade, how would their situation affect her work?

"It's okay. I understand." He stepped back. Her stomach churned anew at this latest side effect. "My job..." She looked away. "I'll give you my resignation, later today." Even as she said the words, the pain doubled. "You don't have to..." He spoke softly but she turned away. "No. I can't...I don't think we can work together after all this." Her eyes burned. She needed something—someone to just take away the pain. Damn it all! She deserved someone to make things right for her. She sighed, knowing he wasn't going anywhere, anytime soon.

"Look, just...can I get dressed first?" She turned back, then waited until he faced her.

"I'll wait for you out here." He stepped through the door. Deanna slumped back onto the bed, letting her head drop to her hands. "What am I going to do, now?" But nothing came to her as she wallowed in her misery.

"Everything okay in there?" His voice came through the door.

She wanted to scream. While he waited out there, there would be no peace. She wasn't really the kind of person who hid from their problems, so she squared her shoulders once again. What was done was done.

Deanna pushed off the bed and headed over to the wardrobe to rifle though her clothes. Whatever she wore today, it would be her figurative armor, she told herself, before finally settling on a business suit. If her choice of attire didn't shoot the message home, then nothing would.

A burning sensation seared his arm as he hissed, wrenching up the sleeve. *What the...*

A round red welt-like mark appeared. Jalil cursed. He knew exactly what that mark meant, but—surely, she would have known? He gazed at the door as the knowledge settled. She probably didn't, taking into account her reaction to his announcement.

The door opened. There she stood, her black hair impeccably tied up, the deep ruby colored suit screamed, keep your distance. He could read in her face that she didn't want this conversation.

He covered his grin by turning around. "Nice place you have. But I think we should find somewhere a little more...public to talk."

Deanna nodded regally as he pushed a little further.

"We can travel by vehicle...or I can take us there."

Her eyes widened slightly at his words, but as he hoped, she was too intrigued to say no. "Let's try your way. But I need to find my bag, first." She looked around, spying the leather tote upside down in the corner of the room, by the door.

She'd obviously not been very happy by the time she got home, but he knew better than to say anything as she kneeled to pick up the items, which had tumbled out.

As she stood, he held out a hand. She silently wound her fingers through his. He opened a portal, taking a quick look around before he stepped through, pulling her with him.

Deanna gasped, "Amazing!" She looked around, and then back as the portal closed behind him. "How do you do that?"

The words, you can do that too, trembled on the tip of his tongue but he restrained the urge, knowing instinctively she would pull away from him. Right now he had her at least, willing to talk.

A small cafe sat ahead and he indicated for her to enter.

"Isn't this a little...public for our discussion?" She stopped, turning slightly as she quirked an elegant eyebrow.

"No. It's a meeting place for those of us with...certain abilities." He grinned as her raspberry colored lips rounded once more. "What would you like? A coffee? Or would you prefer tea?"

"Umm, I'll have a cappuccino, thanks." She stood scanning the small cafe. "Shall I grab a table?"

He nodded as he made his way toward the counter.

"JD! Haven't seen you here for a long time." The demon behind the counter smiled widely.

"I'm here on business." Gaspar nodded, watching over his shoulder. "Very good looking business it is too." Possessiveness rose, but he quelled it. Not now. Gaspar didn't need to know more than he currently guessed and he definitely didn't want a scene.

JD ordered, then paid. Gaspar assuring him that once everything was ready he would deliver the coffees to their table.

He moved slowly, trying to get his jumbled feelings under control. Too soon, he reached their table, pulled out the leather covered wood chair, and sat. "Before we start...I have a question for you?"

Deanna's head cocked slightly to one side. "What?"

"Your parents? Where are they?" He cursed inwardly as she sat back in her chair, letting him know the question had struck a nerve.

"Well now, that's a question I've been asking for most of my life." She shrugged, keeping her face impassive. "I don't know. They left me as a kid on the doorstep of some mission, here. There are files, so I was informed, but I've never bothered to go back and get them." The words were quiet and he could see the hurt beneath.

So, here is the source of her lack of faith in others. Jalil leaned forward. "I think...there is something you need to know." He rolled up his sleeve and her face paled as the red mark on his arm was uncovered. "I'm guessing the reason for this is in those files."

"No. No...I didn't do that." She pointed at the welt, glancing up at him wide-eyed. "I couldn't have..."

"Deanna...you need to trust me. I know you don't feel you can right now. But time is of the essence. If the file is there and it contains something useful...and I hope it does, then that should show you I am trustworthy."

She nodded slowly, looking shell-shocked. He thanked the stars she was quick thinking, it had saved a lot of explanation. He didn't want to push her any further, but if what he believed was right, then the dynamics had changed. They had time. They had time to learn about each other before bonding, because the forty-eight hours only applied if the mate were human, and clearly she wasn't. Of course, she still had to agree to the bonding in the end.

In human-demon bonding, there were so few hours because humans aged and died so fast, he had seen many generations of humans born, live their lives and die, but a demon's life was only limited by their continued use of their ability. For him, existence could be forever so long as he continued to enhance and give pleasure to others. Vicariously or not.

If Deanna was a demon or even part demon, then they needed to find out what ability she had. A sense of urgency filled him. "Deanna, once we're finished here, we should head over to the mission to see the file. Please trust me?"

She opened her mouth, probably to argue but shut it again. She nodded silently.

As their coffees were served, Jalil was careful to hide his mark. It was no one's business but their own, he temporized. He toyed with the sugar on the table while Deanna sipped her coffee, then realized what he was doing, raised the drink once more and downed it swiftly.

As soon as their cups were drained, they rose in silence and walked to the door. "Come again!" called Gaspar. He waved as he ushered her through the door with speed. They hurried along the street while she led the way. Jalil watched the hypnotic sway of her hips, smiling as he remembered the feel of her silky skin beneath his hands. She looked back as if feeling his stare. "Get that look off your face." He laughed, unable to hold in the feeling any longer. "What? What's so funny that you can laugh about this situation?" Her tense words sobered him, as he realized he hadn't explained the change in the situation. "When we get through this, I'll explain everything. If what I hope is in the files is right, then believe me, this whole situation will be so much better." Her eyes betrayed her distrust. He sighed again as she turned away, leading him to a tall dilapidated building hidden behind metal doors. She reached in, turned the latch, and then motioned him forward. "I haven't been back here in years."

CHAPTER EIGHT

Climbing up the steps felt odd to Deanna. In her memories, they loomed bigger and more frightening. Not that anything bad had ever happened to her while living at the mission. But memories of being an orphan, the sense of relying on the kindness of strangers for her continued survival weren't the happiest recollections a girl could have.

Reaching the bright red door, she gripped the old brass knocker. One, two, three thuds filled the air. Somewhere within came the sound of laughter while she waited, tapping her feet on the concrete steps. Footfalls echoed within, and then the door creaked open.

"Hello. How can I..." The voice petered off as the older lady looked at her over the rims of her glasses. "Well now. Deanna! You are a sight for sore eyes!" The woman leaned forward, wrapping wrinkled arms around her waist. "Come in. Come in."

Zrinka, the house mother, pulled her forward through the door, into the cool hallway. "And your friend too."

Deanna turned to see him step in with a smile. "Hello, I'm JD." The woman smiled, blushing slightly while Deanna rolled her eyes, watching him reach out to shake Zrinka's hand. Then he stepped back and the flustered woman's hands moved like bird wings. "Deanna, dear, is there some way we can help you?" "I've...We've come searching for the records that were left here with me." The woman looked at her as if assessing her words, before looking at Jalil, then nodding sagely. "Yes, we expected you would need to see them at some point."

Zrinka indicated the small cramped office. Deanna and Jalil followed her through the doorway before settling with a squeak into the old brown leather and wood seats. Zrinka opened a filing cabinet door and fished around before announcing, "Aha!"

She held up a faded and tattered file, then headed to the scarred desk and sat down. She placed the file before Deanna.

"As with all files, there is a sealed section dealing with how you came to be in our care. None of us know what is in it. Only the person leaving you here knows what they wrote. I do know though, there was a letter as well in the envelope." She shrugged. "Apart from that, your file contains medical records, academic records and incidentals pertaining to your time here."

Deanna looked at the folder. The cardboard was battered and dog-eared, but the fear of what may be inside subsided a little.

"Zrinka, can I—Can you leave me for a while? Just so I can look through the contents by myself."

The woman smiled, nodded and rose. At the door she looked back. "Let me know when you are ready to talk."

Deanna nodded, the hollow in her stomach threatening to overwhelm her. Jalil stood, but she reached out a hand, needing him here, with her. She needed his support. "Stay, please. I want you here."

Without a word he resumed his seat.

Deanna took a deep breath, opening the file. Inside were pages of handwritten notes, sleeves with records. She would read them later. But right now, the information she needed was contained in the letter, hidden in the sealed section.

A hand, gentle and reassuring touched her shoulder. "Take your time."

She opened the sealed section and picked out the white envelope. With shaking fingers, Deanna turned it over. She hadn't been ready for this before, but now the time had arrived. She couldn't avoid it any longer. She broke the dried seal and pulled out the sheet of paper waiting within.

Withdrawing it with care, she chanced a look at Jalil. The look on his face reassured her, while she slowly unfolded the page.

Deanna,

You will be fully grown now. I wish I could have seen you reach maturity. But it could never happen, because while your father is mostly human, I am not. It won't be easy to understand a lot of what you will read here. You may even find it fantastical. But before you read any further, I want you to understand, I made this choice out of love.

I am a demon. A demon of fire. Your father only had a drop of demon blood that is the only way you could be conceived. He seemed unaware of what he was, and I knew he could never be my mate. I thought, at the time, I could dally, but I was wrong.

I digress, forgive me.

You are a demon also. Not fully, but that is your heritage. You need to find what you are, because until you do so, you cannot know true happiness. You may not be a fire demon. We all need to find our own path. I wish I could be there to help you find yours.

But what you do need to know is I could not keep you. My master forbade it. He was right, as I could not keep you safe, either in my service to him or because I remained unmated even though i'd found and been with my One.

I searched to find a safe place for you to grow. They are good people where I leave you, with a reputation for taking children like you in. Of caring for demon children as their own. It is why I chose to place you here.

As for your father, he never knew about you. He died in an accident sometime after you were conceived.

But now as you are reading this, I am thinking it is because you have to make a choice. Don't let the sorrows of your past stop you.

They are just that, the past.

We can have regrets. I know my biggest will be saying goodbye to you. But don't let them cripple you in your future.

Take the opportunities that come and make them worthwhile. Embrace the life you have. Be happy.

Most of all, know I always loved you and always will.

Deanna's eyes burned. Tears began trickling down her face as she traced the words on the page. "She said she loved me." Hands enfolded her from behind.

"She did. If she were a fire demon, then you would have been unsafe. She had a reason for her choice." Lips kissed the top of her head as she sobbed. "I'm a demon. This proves it, doesn't it?" She held up the piece of paper.

"Well, it tells us what she was, but this mark is probably the best indicator of the lot."

Deanna gulped, then snorted wetly. "I guess it is." Her heart still ached, but for the first time she knew what she was. It freed her. "I guess we better look at what else is in the sealed section of the file."

Her hands shook as she reached for the closed folder, but he gripped them. "Together." He spoke gently, his words a caress that soothed the feelings churning and roiling mercilessly within her stomach.

He handed the file over, then she slipped a trembling finger under the seal. She shook the folder upside down. A small medallion dropped free and he laughed.

"What is it?" Her gaze roamed over the old metal as she reached out a hand.

"It's a seal. One I know. It's Elron's seal. He served on Piero, working there until his death. He was a concubine of great repute." She started at his words. Her father had been a server on one of the pleasure planets?

"Hang on, how do you get your abilities?" A sneaking suspicion rose. *Surely not!*

"From one of our parents. You will have an ability either of them possessed. His sister turned out to be a pleasure demon, so you could be too." He grinned. "That would explain the chocolate factory. You've been there, how long?"

"Five years. I started not long after Eric and Sarcha died..." The import of his words hit her. "Holy hell! Was their accident my fault?"

"No! Bonding doesn't work like that, at all. It's more like a case of emptiness that leaves us wanting something more. It's as if you are missing something integral. You felt that with Eric, didn't you?"

At his soft words, she realized she had felt just like that. She had loved him, just had never felt like it was enough to fill the missing parts of herself. Sarcha had been the light of her life, though. If she were brutally honest, her daughter had made up for the lack of connection after their first year of marriage.

For the first time, she realized how she had remembered the past with rose-colored glasses. Deanna allowed herself to see the relationship in a different, more honest light. The thought finally freed the last vestiges of loss and grief.

"You're right. I did." Swift on the realization came the knowledge of how Jalil filled those holes deep within her. The sense of betrayal dissipated, together with their problems. She understood what had driven her all these years. It had been the guilt that kept her tethered to the past.

It also explained his reaction after they had made love. "So, now what?" Another fact hit home. "Oh my God! How long do you have left?"

Jalil smiled. "As much time as we need."

CHAPTER NINE

Deanna smiled at the sight of the table. The months had flown by as he had guided her through the process of learning of her demonhood. He'd introduced her to Elron's family. They were truly her family now.

Jalil had helped her explore her abilities, which were as suspected, those of a pleasure demon. As he'd indicated, they explained why the chocolate company had become more successful after she started working there. Unfortunately, it had already been too late to help Feliz and Alannah. A fact she now accepted as fated.

In the past months, Jalil had proven himself time and again as honest, loving and loyal. They had become as close as two human lovers could be. But tonight...Well tonight, she would seal the deal. Nothing filled her with more happiness than the thought of bonding to him totally.

She wore new silky black underwear and had dressed in a midnight blue gown. Dinner waited in the dining area. The staff had been sent away for the night. Not long after the revelation of her demonhood he had shared the fact he lived at the floating resort.

Now she did too.

Her things mixed with his. Even the photo of Eric and Sarcha had a place in her small home office, tucked away where she could pull it out to look on her life from before. But she didn't do that very often.

Light flared and she smiled. He had finally arrived. She hurried to the dining room, reaching for him with a scorching kiss. "Welcome home. Now leave your things there. Come sit down."

He smiled, even as he quirked an eyebrow with the unspoken question.

Excitement bubbled. She lifted a glass of champagne to her lips. "To us. To tonight. The night we finally bond."

His eyes blazed as he put down the glass and moved toward her. "You mean that?"

She placed her glass on the table feeling his excitement. Now that she had embraced her own nature, she felt so much more deeply than before.

"Yes I do." "Then, why are we waiting? Let's go." He reached her and nuzzled at her neck.

"Not yet. I want to make it as special as we can, for both of us." He sighed deeply, as if put out, but she saw the light in his eyes. "Okay." She laughed at the comical act. "So sit down." Deanna lit the candles on the table before she aimed the remote at the hidden stereo. Soft music filled the air. The meal was exotic, a foreplay without touching, involving tastes and textures that tantalized taste buds. Each song soulfully pulled at them on an emotional level. The candles, which lit the room, flickered as they spoke while each look was filled with promise. She could feel her body becoming aroused well before they reached the dessert course, finishing with the finest chocolates ever made by Scheherazade. The ones she'd named Lovers Desire. Her cheeks flamed as she sipped the aged champagne, then sat the glass down.

They both rose.

This is it.

They moved together, hands clasped tightly as they walked in silence to the bedroom beyond. His look of surprise pleased her as they entered. She had changed the heavy brocade curtains of the room for lace and placed pillar candles on every available surface. With a click of her fingers, the room glowed and he smiled.

"Got that down, haven't you."

"I have indeed." She sashayed closer to him. "So lover boy, what are you going to do now?"

He moved so quickly, she almost missed him. His hands clamped around her waist as his lips found hers, devouring her until he pulled away. "God, but I love you."

Her heart melted at the words. She'd seen the truth of that in his action, but until now, he'd never said them. Triumph coursed through her.

"I love you too." She smiled up at him, pushing closer. She shivered with anticipation. They had discussed what needed to happen to bond them. His hands shook slightly as he reached for the zipper of her dress. "Did I tell you how beautiful you look tonight?" "Not tonight, but just about every morning, noon and evening as well." Her voice shook with emotion.

"Then I was, indeed, remiss. You look exquisite."

His lips met hers, softly at first, firming against hers. His tongue sought entry. She slid her fingers to the tangle of hair at his nape, twining in the luxuriant silk. His mouth trailed along her jaw, nipping here and there. Sensually teasing her while his hands ranged over her body. They found clips and zippers, each touch inflaming her senses as her heart beat a rapid cadence.

Wherever his fingers touched she burned like tinder. Finally the dress slid to the floor. "My, my. What do we have here?" He pulled away, his eyes feasting. "A surprise, ready for you to unwrap." Now she had fully embraced her nature, their lovemaking was deeper. Sheer devilry sparked in his eyes. "I look forward to it." Her fingers moved swiftly then, deftly undoing each button she could find, wanting to touch his skin. He pulled away. "Wait. Let's not rush." His voice was thick with desire. She shuddered as a rush of pleasure invaded her body. "We can do take our time, once I have you naked." He chuckled at her words. "In that case..." Jalil shrugged off his jacket and shirt, letting them drop away. His bare chest called to her, but it wasn't enough. Already unbearably aroused, she panted but was determined to take her time with the pleasure the night would bring. She ran her fingers down her legs, finding the clips of the stockings and flicked them. His eyes flamed. Smiling lightly, she kicked off her shoes.

Jalil bent long enough to shed his own, then the socks beneath.

As her stockings gaped, she knew they caught his eye, by the ruddy flush that flooded his cheeks. He stood before her, still wearing his pants. Her gaze roamed over him, she wanted more. "Take them off."

He smirked at her. "Take what off?" "Take the rest of your clothes off. I want to see you naked. Every. Single. Inch." He assumed a pose and she snickered, though it died away as his hands moved to the clips, buttons and zippers, tearing at them. Her breath fled as he finally stood naked in front of her. His erection jutted proudly from his body. When a small bead of moisture glistened on the end of the head she sucked in a breath. She warmed further, as her breasts engorged, nipples peaking beneath the confines of the silk.

She reached for her bra clips, but he shook his head. "I'll do that."

Moving forward, he slipped his arms under her legs and

lifted her to the bed. The mattress dipped under their combined weight as he kneeled beside her.

"I get to open my present now." His lips found hers once more as his clever hands firmed over her breasts. They tingled while the pleasure singed her. She mewled slightly in the back of her throat and he smiled.

"There is so much more pleasure to come tonight. I'm going to love you as you've never been loved before."

"Oh Jalil!" Her throaty cries spurred him on, as he kneaded her breasts. They swelled further in response. Her nipples were sensitive as they rubbed against the material of her bra.

Jalil slipped one finger below the silky satin to the distended tip, toying with the nub until she cried out, knees shaking.

The other hand grazed the flesh of her belly, leaving trailing tongues of fire before it burrowed into her panties, finding the damp curls hidden below. His fingers found the sensitive folds and lightly touched but then moved away from her throbbing core while his other hand continued the sensual exploration of her breasts.

Each touch and stroke fanned the fire that grew within her.

He crooned as she thrashed in her need, while her heart beat a rapid tattoo. She clawed at him, her fingers seeking purchase on his slick skin but he pulled away each time they moved toward his erection.

He lifted himself away, disentangling his hands from beneath her underwear, breathing heavily. "Slow down. We have to slow down." His chest heaved as he struggled to find the words. "Sit up." With shaking arms, she managed. He reached behind her, removed the strapless bra, and then threw it over his shoulder. Her breasts sagged slightly once the support was gone, the cool air caressing her heated skin. She shivered in reaction.

"Beautiful. Simply beautiful." His muttered words were lost on her as his stare roamed over her nearly naked form and her nipples puckered harder.

His fingers slid down her back, unhurriedly, finding each indentation as he murmured, "I'm going to eat you up, lick every inch of your body, then make you scream with pleasure."

She quavered deep inside at his darkly sensual words. Finally his hands slipped below her panties once more. He tugged them down her legs, baring her totally to his gaze.

With one firm hand, he pushed her back to the bed, supine, before inching her legs apart. His gaze burned as he leaned forward, so slowly. Each second making her ache more for his touch.

He slipped a finger across her aching core, dipping slightly so they were coated with her moisture. Then they moved away, only to retrace the pattern again and again, each pass ratcheting up her need while her heart pounded.

He leaned forward, his tongue touched her sensitive flesh, teasing the nubbin and she jerked at the pleasure that speared through her system. "I'm not going to...be able to hold on...if you do that."

Her broken words didn't stop him though, he stilled for an instant, then smiled. "That's my plan."

He bent farther over, his hands holding her legs captive as he lapped and sucked on her, his tongue invading the secret recesses while she jerked and shuddered. Her fingers caught in the sheets, twisting them as she fought the invading pleasure.

Pleasure tore through her as she orgasmed, violently shuddering apart in his arms.

Roughly, Jalil captured her in his arms and hauled her

toward him. "Now. Now we mate!" His skin changed to the mottled blue and green, but this time she had no qualms as he centered himself between her legs. With one hard thrust, he sank home. She cried out again, the feel of him sliding within her body, bringing a sense of triumph.

"Now!" His arms circled her.

She knew instinctively that this was the moment. The instant of change was upon her, while her body moved sinuously. Her skin shades of violet as their true beings came together for the first time.

"I bond with you!" Her broken cry matched his, word for word. They shuddered together, feeling the magic overcoming them. She continued to undulate caught up in her passion, hips moving in the ancient rhythm as he thrust within her molten core.

Another wave of pleasure swamped her, the orgasm this time was deeper than the last, the exquisite milking sensation so overwhelming she cried out.

They tensed in each other's arms, welcoming the bonding, as the magical connection flowed between them. They held onto each other while their bodies calmed and skin resumed the human creaminess that they'd inhabited in the outside world.

"Damn. That was good." He chuckled.

Deanna snorted. Right now, she felt so alive and energized. As she'd never before. With a wink, she drawled, "Wanna do it again?"

Did you enjoy The Chocolate Affair? If so, why not take a look at some more of Imogene's Books?
Flip on for some teasers!

Click on the image and sign up to my newsletter!
Terms & Conditions can be found on my website
www.imogenenix.net

Can a cyber-enhanced warrior and a ship's captain find love together?

Levia Endrado never wanted to be a warrior, but at seventeen she was deemed suitable for battle. After intense training and multiple enhancements, which gave her superior strength and healing ability, she was sent off to defeat the enemy—a killing machine with a mission.

When the war was over, she had to find a new life. At twenty-seven she's a washed-up veteran without a future. Or she was, until she met Sandon Daria.

Serving as a pilot aboard Sandon's spaceship the *Golden Echo* makes Levia long for a different and gentler life. But old hurts and even older enemies aren't so easily forgotten. Particularly when they come back for her.

Sandon is determined to show Levia that she's more than just a BioCybe...she's the woman who completes him. Getting close is just the first step, keeping her alive is an even bigger challenge, but one he's willing to take because the prize is their combined future.

Levia scanned the long line of other hopefuls entering the chamber. The large building in the center of town was cold, and she dragged her wrap around her body, even as she craned her head, looking to the high ceiling. She'd never before had an occasion to enter the testing complex, yet she'd seen the lines of teenagers every time they passed the building.

Once she'd asked her parents why the teens were lined up and her mother's face had shuttered. Her stepfather had just shaken his head and growled. They'd stopped her questions with a carefully uttered, "You'll know soon enough, Levia." The pain in her mother's eyes had been enough to shush her questions. For endless months afterward, her parents had traveled different routes to the educational facility she attended and Levia lost interest in the puzzle of that building.

Now, as she looked around, remembering that long ago spring day, it was her opportunity to find out. But she felt a surge of concern at what lay ahead. She likely wasn't the only one, given that there were probably two to three hundred seventeen-year-olds gathered in the one place. Ahead of her, she caught sight of a couple of girls, their arms linked together and wide smiles on their faces. Scanning the crowd, she became aware that, by far, a majority of those gathered displayed both fear and trepidation.

"All female subjects will enter through doors three, six, and seven. All male subjects will enter through gates four, eight, and ten." The speaker above her was loud, and she jumped before checking the numbers etched on the black metal sign over her head.

The massive doors beside her swung open, and now an uncertain silence reigned. Many of the youngsters hung back, clearly discomforted by whatever testing regime lay ahead. This was where they'd been told their futures would be determined.

"Oh gosh, I hope they only have an aptitude and psych eval. I don't think..." Levia turned to see the white face of the girl behind her. The girl had uttered what many must silently be thinking.

Levia dragged an unsteady breath in, her hand resting flat against the plane of her belly as she looked around. No one had entered yet. It was clear many were on the verge of taking the step, but still they hung back.

She straightened her shoulders. "I'm not afraid." It was always wiser to approach things head-on, she believed. When her biological father had died, she'd been one of the few to view his capsule before it was sent into the massive gray structure built to accommodate those who'd moved onto the next life realm.

Her legs shook as she wobbled toward the entrance.

Beyond the doorway, she spied sealed cubicles and her heart stuttered. Why cubicles? Usually testing—med and psych—were in eval-units, hidden only by billowing white curtains. She glanced back, noting that others had taken the first step.

"Move along, subjects." Once again, the androgynous voice of the address system blared.

Of course, given it was her seventeenth anniversary of birth, she was technically considered an adult now.

She thought longingly of baby Rald and her half-sister, Elda, waiting at home for her to return, and the celebrations to be held that night. That made her smile. She would need to make them proud of her.

She entered a row and the tall Educational Specialist, the edu-specs as her peers laughingly called them, stopped her. "Present your credentials to the scanner."

She'd done this many times since the tiny implant had been slipped below the dermal layer of her skin at birth. The small unit in her wrist heated as her details were checked.

"Enter the first cubicle, Levia Endrado, and follow the instructions to complete your assessment."

Thus dismissed, Levia moved to the first unit, laid her palm against the scanner, and the door slid open soundlessly.

"Welcome, Levia Endrado. Take your place in the eval-unit." The soft contralto of the voice echoed after the door closed silently behind her.

"What are you evaluating?" Her voice was breathy, and she peered around.

"Your skills—physical and psychological. Your emotional and medical status. Your educational attainment levels."

It was an answer that shed little insight into the many things she was hungry to know. "Why do all seventeen year olds—" "Take a seat, Levia. Then we may begin your testing." If she'd expected an answer, she was sadly mistaken, she considered sourly. She dropped into the seat, the soft leather-like surface molding to her body. "Levia Endrado, you are required to remove all non-specified apparel." She jolted in the chair. "It's cold." "The temperature will be amended. Remove the non-specified apparel." Her misgivings grew as she dragged off the light wrap she'd brought with her, and then threw it to the floor at the side of the unit. "We will begin, Levia Endrado. At any time, should you experience any malfunctions of the unit, simply depress the red button." It glowed and she grimaced. Levia reclined against the chair and waited for the testing to begin. The first examination was based on her understanding of the political system, where she saw herself, and her knowledge of the rights and responsibilities accorded through citizenship of both her planet and the commonwealth.

The second test was mathematical and scientific proficiency. It felt like hours had passed by the time she'd finished, and she lay limp on the seat, exhausted.

"Levia Endrado, you may rise. The sanitary unit will emerge once you trigger the yellow button at the door. Should you require refreshment, press the blue button and a restorative will be made available."

"Can I leave?" "Negative, Levia Endrado. Your needs will be catered for in this capsule." "Why?" Her voice hitched and true fear rose for the first time. Why did they keep her in the alcove? "All will be revealed at the end of the testing cycle." Levia looked at the now empty screen before hurling a curse word. It was met with silence. The urgent throb of her bladder reminded her that she needed to use the facilities, so, with

a sigh, she rose and clambered from the seat. After attending to the needs of her body, she walked around the unit, peering at the door, but it was obviously programmed remotely. She poked and prodded, but it made no difference. With a huff, she headed back to the chair.

The moment she'd settled in, the viewing screen shone bright. "Welcome back, Levia. The next sequence will evaluate your psychological reflexes, then that will be followed up with the general knowledge portion of the evaluation."

"When can I leave?" It seemed better to ask bluntly, she told herself.

"Once the examination is completed. After the next set of evaluations, you will be subjected to the physical aspect."

"Then I can go home?"

"Levia Endrado, you will now complete the psychological test. This will be undertaken by one of the center's personal evaluators."

She frowned. Personal evaluators? She bit her lip, and the sting reminded her that this wasn't something to joke about. In her seventeen years, she'd only heard of personal evaluators being brought in once before, and that was when one of the girls at her academy had been in a serious accident. Both legs were amputated and her body's ability to keep her alive had been gravely compromised. Her peers had been informed that the girl had requested the assessment before she could request her support systems be disconnected.

"Levia Endrado, are you ready to recommence processing?" The emotionless voice echoed once more and she gulped.

"Yes."

In the darkness evil waits…

As a young bride Kira was whisked away from everything and

everyone she knew, including her new husband and became Christina, an operative of the Displaced Persons Unit.

As the danger grows she sees an opportunity to save her husband Vasya and sister Serina. But nothing is the same. Serina is grown up—married and pregnant.

Vasya too is older and darkly forbidding. Trusting Christina doesn't come easily until a catastrophic event takes place. Now, knowing the truth everything he thought he knew is changed. But at a very high cost.

The four must work together to defeat the Demon, Zuor and the stakes are higher than they imagined and all could be lost.

The burning at the back of her neck warned she was being watched. A quick glance didn't clarify it. Instead, she turned around in time to see her mother's face, pale. "Mama?" She took a step forward, but her grandfather snatched her wrist.

The grip was painful, and Kira stilled. "Let your parents talk."

She didn't know what the topic of conversation was, but it couldn't be good.

The dappled sunlight seemed cooler than before.

Her father crooked his forefinger at her grandfather while they stood there. For a moment she wished Vasya had come with them, but he had to work. Just the thought of her new husband warmed Kira.

She only had a few minutes to contemplate her newly defined status as a married woman, when her grandfather pulled at her hand. "Come with me." He tugged and, confused, Kira allowed herself to be towed away.

A glance at her parents' faces stole any feeling of well-being. "Grandfather?"

"Shh, my love. You must go." His grip was implacable and his face stern, but he shivered.

"What are you doing? Where are you taking me, Grandfather?"

They moved rapidly through the village they'd visited to sell their wares just that morning, and for the first time since they'd arrived in the market place she felt fear. What was wrong? Was it something to do with Vasya?

"You are in danger. We must send you away." The words confused her further. Send her away? Danger?

"Where is Vasya?" She stumbled over a stone, but he kept tugging her onwards.

With a quick glance around, he hauled her into a dirty laneway between the buildings. Kira gasped, trying to drag air into her starving lungs. "There's no time. We must get you away."

A nondescript shopfront lay ahead, and he pushed on the door. It rattled and opened with a loud groan. "Andre? Andre, are you here?"

An older man shuffled into the room, bent nearly double from the weight of the load on his back. "Marat? What do you want?"

"My granddaughter. They are coming for her and us. Get her away. Take her now, while you can."

The man's face clouded over. "Are you sure?"

"Grandfather, where is Vasya?" Fright had the blood in her veins pounding.

"Hush, my precious. Andre will see you well." He turned. "Whatever it takes, Andre. Take her now." With surprising speed, her grandfather whirled and was gone.

The man, Andre, eyed her. "Come this way, child. There is no time to be lost."

Eleven years later

The tattoo of her heart and cry of terror woke her, as they usually did. Once again, as she had since that rapid flight from those who sought her, she found herself in a lonely bed.

Hundreds of miles away from everything she'd dreamed of, in a house she'd built for them to share. As always, it left her wishing that Vasya had fled with her.

Instead, here she was, exiled without her husband. With a sob, she rolled over and let the tears fall.

Available from Most Online Bookstores
books2read.com/IOTB

Direct Autographed Copy
http://bit.ly/2w6g4K6

Imogene is published in a range of romance genres including Paranormal, Science Fiction and Contemporary. She is mainly published in the UK and USA and is slowly re-releasing her back catalogue, including titles that will be first time in print!

In 2011, Imogene Nix (the pen name not Imogene herself) was born. Imogene sat down and worked tirelessly for 3 months culminating in the books Starline, which became the first in a trilogy titled, "Warriors of the Elector."

Imogene has successfully been contracted for twenty-five titles. She has also completed several others. In 2017 Imogene decided to self publish most of her further works - a plan which is in train.

Imogene is a member of a range of professional organisations world wide, and believes in the mantra of mentoring and paying it forward.

She loves to drink coffee, wine & eat chocolate and is parenting 2 spoiled dogs and a ferocious cat along with her husband and 2 human daughters.

To Contact Imogene
www.imogenenix.net

imogene@imogenenix.net

ALSO BY IMOGENE NIX

<u>Warriors of the Elector</u>

- Star of Ishtar
- Starline
- Starfire
- Star of the Fleet
- Starburst
- The Star of Eternity

The Star of Ishtar & Starline - Print

Starfire & Star of the Fleet - Print

Starburst & The Star of Eternity - Print

<u>Blood Secrets</u>

- The Blood Bride
- The Illuminated Witch
- The Sorcerer's Touch

<u>The Search Duology</u>

- Miss Elspeth's Desire
- Miss Isabelle's Craving (Not Yet Released)

<u>Reunion Trilogy</u>

- War's End
- The Assassin
- Executing Justice

The Reunion Trilogy in Paperback

<u>Sex Love & Aliens</u>

- Tangled Webs
- False Webs
- Covert Webs

<u>21st Testing Protocol</u>

- Cyborg: Redux (Not Yet Released)
- Children Of A Greater Evil (Not Yet Released)
- When Evil Came To Stay (Not Yet Released)
- Finis: The War To End All Wars (Not Yet Released)

<u>Celtic Cupid Trilogy</u>

- Blame The Wine
- A Stranger's Embrace
- Revenge On Cupid

<u>Single Titles</u>

The Chocolate Affair

A Sapphire for Karina

BioCybe

Hesparia's Tears

Tomorrow's Promise

A Bar In Paris

Inheritance Of The Blood

The Plan

Loving Memories

The Reset (2018)

Hero of Heartbreak Hill

Raspberry Dreams (Not Yet Released)

Non Fiction

Self Publishing: Absolute Beginners Guide (With Suzi Love)

Written as Ciara Cave

25 Curated Ways To Get Rid Of Telemarketers

Book Signings for Absolute Beginners